LOST ANGEL

AND OTHER STORIES

WRITTEN BY

TIANA DORA NONGKHLAW

Copyright ©2020 Tiana Dora Nongkhlaw

"Lost Angel and other stories," published through Young Author Academy.

Young Author Academy LLC

Dubai, United Arab Emirates

www.youngauthoracademy.com

ISBN: 9798711335146

Printed by Amazon Direct Publishing.

Tiana would like to thank her family, friends, Annemieke from Young Author Academy, everyone at The Hive and all the teachers at her school for their guidance and support.

The book "Lost Angel and other Stories," is her first published work, and she hopes that children of all ages will enjoy reading it.

- Contents -

Lost Angel

Lost Angel

Once upon a time in a small village, there stood a little cottage where a girl named Gale lived with her parents. She liked reading adventure books and drawing pictures of the animals in the forest she had seen and made friends with. Gale loved caring for animals and every day she would go to the forest and care for the animals that lived there.

One day when she was visiting the forest, Gale heard a strange sound. She thought the sound was very familiar, but she couldn't quite put her finger on it.

So Gale went in the direction of where the sound was coming from and as she moved closer, she realised the sound that she heard was of a person crying.

The sound seemed to come from behind the tall trees. She looked behind them and saw a little boy.

"Why are you crying?" she asked him.

"I was playing with my dog, Angel, when she suddenly barked and ran off deep into the forest. I tried to follow her but she continued to run and I myself, became lost in this forest," he cried.

Gale comforted the boy and said, "It's okay. How about I take you home and I'll come right back to find Angel. Once I find her, I will bring her home to you."

The boy nodded. So she took him home and went straight back to the forest in search of Angel.

"I wonder if she left any footprints. Well, not footprints so to speak, but paw prints," Gale said to herself. She went back to the place where she found the boy and patiently started to hunt for paw prints.

Finally, her patience was rewarded. She found a long trail of paw prints. She followed the paw prints until they came to a sudden stop.

"She must have left some other clue," she said.

Gale continued to search for the missing pup. After searching for a few minutes, she felt thirsty, so she sat down under the shade of a tree to rest. She took out a water bottle from her backpack and began to drink. She found it quite uncomfortable to drink with her backpack on, so she took it off and placed it on the ground beside her.

She rested for a while and began to think, 'Angel could be anywhere in this forest,' she thought. 'A map would be very useful right now.'

Then she was struck with an idea. She could make her own map! She had been to the forest enough times to remember it by memory.

She hadn't been to all the places in the forest, but she had studied other maps of it. Too bad she didn't have them with her on this occasion.

Gale looked in her backpack and found some white chart paper and some pens, and pencils and erasers in her pencil pouch. She then began to draw her map. She had already drawn maps before in school for her projects, so drawing a map of the forest wasn't so difficult.

Twenty minutes later, she had finished drawing her map. It showed the whole forest in detail.

She had also written the names of the places that she knew of on her new map.

Gale got up and reached for her backpack. With her eyes still fixed on the map, and with her hands, she reached for her backpack, however, she couldn't find it. She turned away from the map and to her surprise, her backpack was missing! She looked all around but she couldn't find it.

Then something unusual happened. A pen fell on her head from the tree above. It didn't hurt, but it surprised her enough to make her look up. And guess who was there? It was Trouble! .... with Gale's backpack!

Trouble was a monkey that Gale had once saved from an angry snake. The snake had chased Trouble because he had stepped on the snake's tail. Luckily, the snake chased Trouble all the way to Gale's house and she was able to take him in before the snake had caught up to him.

This incident had given Gale the idea to name him Trouble, because of the trouble that he was always causing. Now, he was there on the branch with Gale's backpack.

"Trouble! Come on down and give me the backpack, please," she said gently, but instead of coming down, he climbed up the tree even higher!

Gale huffed. Asking never really worked for monkeys as it had for a few other animals. Then Gale had another idea. Trouble always enjoyed playing the imitation game! The game that Gale created herself, where he would copy anything that Gale did. As in, when Gale clapped her hands, Trouble would do the same. Gale thought that if she dropped something, then perhaps Trouble would copy her and drop her backpack!

She took out her handkerchief and said, "Come on Trouble, Game Time! Game time!"

Trouble tilted his head with a clear look of confusion. Gale dropped her handkerchief. Trouble chittered something and then low and behold, he dropped Gale's backpack.

"Yes!" shrieked Gale, as she caught the backpack just before it hit the ground.

She slung it around her shoulders before Trouble had the chance to pick it up again. She reached into her waist-pouch and took out a banana.

She threw it to Trouble who caught it with ease. He chittered with delight and then left.

After Gale was done making sure that the map was perfectly drawn, she started to look for more clues for where she could find the little boy's missing dog, Angel.

Gale suddenly noticed something unusual in front of her. The grass around her was long and immensely straight, but when she looked closer, she saw that some of the grass away from her was crooked and bent, like something had trodden on it.

'Maybe it was Angel!' she thought.

Gale followed the flattened grass that led her to a deep mud pit.

"Oh dear," she said, "It wasn't Angel who made the grass bent after all."

She was just turning back when she heard a bark. It wasn't coming from behind her, it was coming from the mud pit.

"Angel!" Gale shouted. Then she saw a small dog sinking in the mud pit. She quickly took action.

She grabbed some vines and made a lasso and threw it to Angel.

"Missed!" she said and threw it again.

"Yes!" she shouted as the lasso fell right over Angel's waist.

She tugged at the lasso and Angel floated towards her. Gale picked her up and examined her to see if she was hurt. She seemed fine, only a bit muddy. After Gale had wiped Angel clean, with some tissues from her backpack, she and Angel made their way back home to the little boy, using the map.

The boy was so happy when he saw Gale walking up his pathway with his precious Angel in her arms.

"Oh, thank you ever so much for finding my dog. How did you find her?" The little boy asked when Gale handed over Angel to him.

"Well!" Gale said, "Let's just say... it was quite an adventure."

The Friendly Dragon

THE FRIENDLY DRAGON

Once upon a time there was a very friendly dragon who loved to help others. The dragon's name was Spikes. Now, for a dragon, Spikes was very kind and gentle. Dragons are usually mean, unkind and violent, always stealing food and hurting other creatures, but Spikes was different. He cared for the animals of the forest and he had never stolen anything in his entire life. He even considered himself a vegetarian and a protector of the animals.

Now, the other dragons didn't like Spikes. Not one little bit, because of his kind nature, and they always tried to make him behave like a real dragon and not just to look like one, but Spikes never listened to them.

Whenever they did try to make him behave like a real dragon, he would just turn away and say, "I am happy just the way I am with my animal friends in my cave. I would never sacrifice my happiness or my friend's happiness for the sake of 'acting' like a 'real' dragon. I'm already real enough to see that if I listen to you I would also be wasting my time." So, with that, the dragon's didn't disturb him anymore.

One day, the dragons were out hunting, when they saw a deer, perfect for their catch. Their leader ordered them to surround the deer quietly in order not to startle the animal, otherwise it would run away. They were just about to pounce upon the deer when something happened. First, the deer just disappeared. Then they heard a mighty roar overhead and above them they saw a dragon soaring. It was Spikes! Spikes swiftly landed amongst the herd dragons with the deer held firmly, but safely in his claws.

"So, do you finally agree to be a non-vegetarian like you're supposed to be, eh Spikes?" said the dragon leader, Zeke.

"No, I was trying to save this deer from you and your group. You can take any animal from this forest, but you keep away from my friends," replied Spikes.

Zeke's eyes glinted angrily, "How can we hunt animals that are not your friends, when you are friends with absolutely everyone in the whole forest? We shall starve to death if this irrational behaviour continues!" He shouted.

But Spikes remained calm and responded, "You could try eating fruits and vegetables. I can give you some of my vegetable soup and carrot cake for desert. It's kind of my specialty you know?"

Zeke shook his head, "You sometimes forget that you are the only dragon in history to ever be vegetarian," snapped Zeke.

"Well, it doesn't mean that I can't be the first one!" snapped back Spikes. "Look! Let's not do anything rash. I offered you my food because you said that you were hungry, but you didn't accept it, so unless you accept my food, I don't know what to do."

Zeke huffed, "Fine, I'll think about it but you really have to start being more dragon-like. Oh, and uh, before I forget, we will stop eating your friends under one condition! Come to the Dragon lair tomorrow and meet me in my office so that we can make an agreement. It's either that, or we continue to eat your animal's day after day," he said with a sly grin.

Spikes looked worried for a while and then he nodded his head and looked at Zeke. "It's a deal!" Spikes said. He then flew away with his strong wings flapping against the breeze.

When Spikes reached his cave near the top of a mountain, he started to think and recount his conversation with Zeke. "Zeke told me to come to the dragon lair tomorrow for some agreement or he will keep on leading the hunt to my friends. I agreed to go and now I have to go to the dragon lair tomorrow," he said to himself glumly. 'No doubt this will lead to no good.' He was such in deep thought that he almost forgot that he still had the deer clenched in his claws.

He didn't notice anything until the deer made a scared sound and suddenly Spikes dropped it.

"Oops! Sorry, I forgot that I brought you with me. By the way, Welcome to your new home!" he said excitedly to the deer. "Follow me, I have a few other deers living in my cave. You can make friends with them."

Spikes led the deer to a corner of the cave where there was a rock jutting out slightly blocking a walkway. They both walked behind it and found that it was hiding the entrance to another cave, slightly smaller than the original one. Inside the cave were a few other deer relaxing in the coolness of the underground shelter. There was a drinking bowl at the corner of the cave. It was made of rock, crafted beautifully by Spike's flame. The water inside was provided by a huge bag that was right over the drinking bowl. It had a hole in it, collecting rainwater through the hole through the top of the cave. The hole in the bag dripped the water into the drinking bowl so that the deer always had water available to drink.

Spikes led the deer inside and made sure that he was comfortable. Then he went back to his own cave and went to sleep.

The next morning was bright and sunny. Spikes took out a bag that was given to him on his birthday by his aunt. Spikes always took it out when he would venture out into the forest, just in case he should find a wounded animal that he should take home and care for. If the animal needed immediate care, Spikes had everything in the bag, already prepared - If you're not counting the bed that Spikes used to treat his patients, because that was obviously too big for him to carry around!

Spikes packed the rest of the things that he thought he might need and he set off for the dragon lair. He landed near a big oak tree near the forest and knocked three times on the dragon lair's trunk.

"Password?" came a voice which seemed to come from under the tree.

"Romy founded picker ten and danced with delight under tree loud," recited Spikes. He had always thought it was a very silly password, but didn't say anything in case he caused any offence.

The voice did not respond, but suddenly the ground split open from under Spike's feet and he fell down into the earth. He had just enough time to flap his wings and break his fall into a large underground cave. It appeared to have many smaller caves inside. This was the Dragon Lair.

The Dragon Lair had many items of furniture inside and many other things. Dragons rushed to-and-fro in and out of the caves. Spikes found a cave marked 'Leaders.' He slowly crept inside and found some more even tinier caves. The only difference was that these caves had wooden doors. He wandered around until he found a door marked, 'Hunting group leader.'

Spikes walked inside and found Zeke sitting on a chair. He was staring at a map of the forest.

When Zeke noticed that he was not alone, he turned to Spikes and said, "Ah, so you made it after all."

Spikes said with a wicked smile, "Yeah, I made it all right. After wandering through this endless maze you call a lair," said Spikes. Usually he would never say it like that. He was a polite dragon, but after wandering around for so long, he wasn't feeling polite.

"What do you want Zeke?" he said.

"Oh, nothing much! I just called you here to ask you to join the hunting team."

"Are you crazy? You know I would never agree to that," bellowed Spikes.

"Yes, I know! But with your animal friends at risk, I was sure you would agree," replied Zeke.

Spikes stared at him in disbelief and finally he said, "I need some time to think about this."

Zeke nodded and pointed to a door near his desk. "Take your time, I want you to think this through properly," he said.

Spikes opened the door and walked inside. The cave behind it was small and dark. He sat on the floor and closed the door behind him and began to think, 'Why would Zeke want me as a hunter when he knows that I'm a horrible hunter, unless there is another side of the story,' thought Spikes. 'What type of a dragon does he think I am? A silly Tor-. Wait a minute, I'm a Ferocious Fire Wing dragon! Of course! My kind is one of the most feared dragons in the land, for our fire. That's why Zeke wants me to join the hunt. Because of my fire! If I could learn to use my fire properly and join the hunt, it would be unstoppable. I know what I need to do to stop them from hurting my friends,' thought Spikes excitedly.

"I need to get out of here, gather all of my animal friends and start a journey beyond my hometown: The Fire Wing Kingdom! All dragons are afraid to go beyond it or even near it but I'm also a Fire Wing, so I'm allowed to go there and everyone with me will be under my protection. No dragon there can kill anyone that is under their own kind's protection. So .... We'll finally be safe!' he thought.

Spikes stood up and opened the door. He told Zeke that he would be interested in joining the hunt. Zeke was a little surprised at first, but soon enough, he just nodded and said, "Brilliant choice! Now go to the counter at the end of the hall and sign up for the hunt; group no. 10 and then meet me and the rest of the group next Friday," he said.

Spikes left the room very solemnly. No one would guess that he was just pretending! As soon as Spikes was out of the room and was done closing the door, he dashed out of the Dragon Lair and quickly went to the bus stop. He got 49 tickets for his animals and flew back to his cave. He didn't have much time; The Fire Wing Kingdom was far away and he only had three days to reach there, before all of the dragons from the hunt would come after him.

When he finally went back to his cave, Spikes quickly packed some things and bundled them in a big curtain. He tied them together with a lot of pins, since he didn't have a suitcase, and gathered up all of his friends. He took them to the bus stop and then put them inside of two buses. He hopped onto the bus himself and then left.

The journey was long and rough, but they made it, and when they reached their destination, they found some beautiful land just outside the kingdom. They found a wonderful cave in a green forest for them to live in and they lived happily ever after.

From that day on, you can be sure that no one ever told Spikes that he needed to be more like a real dragon again.

The Cat with no Tail

The Cat with No Tail

Once upon a time, there was a very greedy cat whose name was Puss. Puss would eat all of his master's goldfish. He would fish out of his neighbour's ponds and if he could steal some more fish, he would!

Now, all of the cats would call Puss names and make fun of him because he was so greedy. But instead of turning over a new leaf, he would think, "The other cats are silly to think that I am greedy. If I'm hungry, I should eat. And what would master do with dumb goldfish? Goldfish are made to eat, right? If I want to eat some of those fish, I should eat!"

So, whenever the other cats tried to talk some sense into him, he would just turn around and say, "Doesn't sound like the cat I know!"

Puss kept on doing this until the other cats became so tired that they just gave up. Now somehow the other cats found out there was a circus coming to town, and told Puss.

Puss thought about it and became very excited. He wasn't excited to go to the circus, but when his master went to the circus, he could have as much fish as he wanted from the kitchen! What a sneak!

So, when his master left for the circus, Puss quickly ran to the kitchen and began to hunt for some fish and he found some on the shelf. The cook had just bought it from the market that evening. She hadn't had enough time to wash and clean it so she kept it on the shelf and planned to clean it later.

Puss ripped off the plastic and the wrapper to the fish that was not his and ate the fish inside. He hadn't finished eating his fish when he smelled a tempting smell in the air. It was the smell of goldfish!

The smell seemed to be coming from his Master's bedroom but Puss wasn't allowed to go in there. 'If there was goldfish in that bedroom,' Puss thought, 'that is exactly where I am going.'

Puss entered the bedroom. The blinds were drawn so the room was very, very dark. He roamed around the room, even despite there being no light, so he kept bumping into stuff. He kept on roaming around blindly until he bumped into a table. Puss jumped onto the table and felt something made of glass brush along his fur.

He grew very excited, 'This must be the fishbowl with the goldfish in it. If only I had some light, I could jump in and catch it,' Puss thought to himself.

Puss couldn't look for the goldfish in the fishbowl without any light or he might tip it over and spill all of the water on himself, and like most cats, Puss hated getting wet. He couldn't reach the light switch because it was too high and he obviously couldn't open the blinds. So, what could he do?

Then he remembered something! Master always hated when the lights suddenly went off when he was doing some important work and he didn't have any light to see, so he bought a special light that didn't require any electricity to operate. It also came with a remote that could switch the special light on and off with a press of a button.

Puss' Master had kept the remote on his desk; exactly where Puss was standing. So, he looked for the remote and found it, he felt around it and found a single button, he pressed it and immediately the light came on.

Puss was happy that he could see his surroundings again but he was most excited to see the fishbowl with three big goldfish. Puss was just about to catch a goldfish when he noticed something, two of the goldfish were just like any other goldfish, but one of them was not. It somehow seemed to glow and shine. Its fins and tail looked like they'd been sprayed with golden glitter. In fact, it looked fantastic. Any other cat would turn away and leave, letting the beautiful creature live, but not Puss. He instantly thought the better it looked, the better it would taste.

Puss put his paw into the fishbowl and swooped for the goldfish. He missed, so he swooped again. He couldn't catch the goldfish but he kept on trying. He was so focused on the goldfish that he didn't hear people talking as they were walking up the pathway towards the house. He didn't hear them unlocking the door and entering. He couldn't hear a thing until the cook screamed loudly from the kitchen.

'What? back already? But I haven't caught my goldfish yet, I have to catch at least one.' Puss thought to himself. By now Puss was frustrated, and he gave one more swoop and, "Yes! I got it!"

Puss was holding the poor goldfish in the water by its tail. While the fish was tugging on its tail trying to get free from Puss, a little part of its tail tore apart. Puss yowled as a spray of water hit him in the face. Soon, Master, the cook and a little man that Puss had not seen before, came running in upon hearing the yowls.

"Oh! Puss you naughty thing. You have eaten Master's magic Goldfish's tail! And…. What a peculiar thing! Your tail is shrinking!" said the cook in a surprised tone.

"Why! You're right! His tail truly is shrinking. It's completely gone now! But how did it happen?" said Master also in a surprised tone.

"Ha! Ha! Ha! Your cat ate a magic goldfish, so the goldfish wanted to teach him a lesson by taking away his tail!" laughed the little man whom Puss didn't know.

"Well then, I can't have a cat with no tail. Shoo! Shoo!" said Master, as he shooed Puss away.

Puss ran out feeling very sorry for himself but then he thought, 'I am so unique now. None of the cats that I know have no tail. So, me not having a tail just makes me special! Oh, how happy am I because now I can also take as much fish as I want from the neighbour's ponds and no one will be there to stop me! Hurrah!"

His happy thoughts soon became louder as he walked on and soon the other cats came running to him upon hearing his, Hurrah!!

"What happened? Did you get another fi- Oh my Puss! You don't have a tail! What happened to it?" asked one of the other cats.

"Well, I lost it and I don't have one anymore, unlike you guys, so that makes me special," said Puss quickly.

The other cats looked at each other and then started to laugh, "Puss thinks he's special because he doesn't have a tail! He doesn't know how ugly he looks without one!" they said.

You should have seen Puss's face then. His face drooped as if all the sorrows of the world rested on his shoulders. Puss ran away thinking about the wrongs of his ways. He thought about them for a long time and soon decided to change them, and he knew exactly where to start. He ran back to the house and went inside with nobody seeing him.

He went straight to the living room where the little man was smoking a pipe. The man noticed Puss immediately and said, "I know exactly what you want. You want to get your tail back and turn over a new leaf but not until you get your tail back," said the little man much to Puss's surprise.

"I'll tell you what you want to know. The only way to get your tail back is to apologize to the goldfish that took it," he said.

As soon as the little man finished his sentence, Puss ran to his master's bedroom and looked inside. No one was there. He padded across the floor and jumped onto the table where the fishbowl was, he looked at the goldfish whose tail he'd bitten and said, "Um, goldfish. Buddy, I am sorry for biting off your tail. I hope you can forgive me," said Puss in an awkward tone.

The fish did not answer but suddenly, Puss's tail grew longer and longer until it was back to its original size. Puss meowed with delight but suddenly regretted it, for Master and the little man came rushing in, "Puss! You've gotten your tail back!" said Master.

"Well, I'll be a monkey's uncle!" said the small man trying his hardest to sound surprised. "Your cat must have apologized to the goldfish and the goldfish must have accepted it."

"Well, if he's a good cat again, I'd be happy to take him back," said Master, beaming.

Puss jumped for joy and he ran to his Master and they lived happily ever after. But you can be sure that Puss never ate another goldfish again.

Mr. Muscle the Toymaker

MR. MUSCLE, THE TOYMAKER

Once upon a time in a forest stood a little hut. In this hut lived a toymaker. The toymaker loved making toys for the children who lived in the village, for he loved them very much and made lots of toys every day, and of course everyone bought them from him.

As time passed, children didn't want his toys anymore because many new modern ones were being invented and his toys were made in a very old style, and they were soon forgotten.

The toymaker was so sad that he moved into the forest instead of living with everyone in the village. He kept on making toys everyday hoping that someone would come to buy them, but he soon lost hope because no one bought his toys.

Little did he know that he was about to become a whole lot happier.

******

"Jane! Johnny! It's time to go!" shouted mother from the car.

"Coming Mom," said Jane and Johnny as they ran out to the car.

They were going on a vacation to the village because they had heard that it was very warm there during the summer. They thought that it would be nice to get away from the noisy, bustling city and retreat to the quiet, peaceful village.

Jane and Johnny got into the car and looked out of the window. "Wouldn't it be marvellous and fun to live in the village? We can explore the forest and run into the fields, collect those smooth stones from the river. We can paint them and we could do so many other things as well!" said Jane excitedly to Johnny.

"I agree. This is going to be a rather exciting time indeed. We could have so many adventures!" replied Johnny equally excited.

"I'm sure you will have wonderful adventures in the village but don't you think it would be good if you rested for a bit? It's a long journey you know," said Johnny's father from the wheel of the car.

After this, there was silence. The rest of the journey was completed in peace. By the time they had reached their destination, it was night-time. They made their way up the stairs of their new home and washed up, ate their dinner and went to bed.

The next morning when Jane and Johnny were done with their breakfast, they decided to explore the forest. "Don't go too deep into the forest or you'll get lost," said their mother to Jane and Johnny, as they made their way to the forest.

"Alright!" they shouted as they were already running down the path.

"Jane, I wonder what we'll find in this forest?" said Johnny as they entered the forest.

"Well, I know exactly what we'll find!" responded Jane.

"What?" asked Johnny looking at Jane.

"Why? adventure of course," said Jane excitedly.

"Yeah, right!" said Johnny.

They talked to each other as they looked around the forest, admiring its beauty. They kept on walking until Jane spotted something. "Hey! Is that a house I see over there?" she said to Johnny pointing in the direction of a house amongst the forest.

"You're right!" answered Johnny looking surprised. "I didn't know someone lived in the middle of the forest," he said.

Then, an old man came out of the house. He went into a shed near the trees. Jane and Johnny watched him from behind a few bushes.

"Jane," whispered Johnny, "Do you think we should go now?" he said.

"Yes," responded Jane in a whisper.

They were just about to leave when they heard a loud crash. They looked behind them and saw that the old man had been carrying some wood but had dropped some pieces and it was now strewn along the grass. The old man started to pick up the pieces from the grass.

"I say Johnny, don't you think we should help him pick up the wood?" said Jane quietly.

"Yeah, I think we should," replied Johnny.

So, they ran to the old man and wasn't he surprised to see them. "Hello there, what are you doing here so deep into the forest" he asked them when they reached him.

"Oh, we didn't realize that we were so deep in the forest sir. We were exploring the forest when we saw your house. We also saw you drop pieces of wood onto the ground so we came to help you pick it up," replied Jane and Johnny.

"Well, thank you ever so much," thanked the old man picking up the wood closest to him.

"We should better go back home now or mother will be worried," said Johnny when he and Jane had finished helping the old man pick up the wood.

"You're going already? Oh, well, at least come into my house. I want to give you something for helping me pick up my wood," said the old man. Jane and Johnny looked at each other, "Okay, I guess we can stay a bit longer," they replied.

The old man grinned and led them to his house and what a surprise that Jane and Johnny had when they entered. There was a table in the middle of the room with a couple of tools on it, but that was not the surprise that they had expected.

The old man took them to a room in the corner of the house and there, was the very room filled with tons and tons of toys just stacked on top of each other.

There were dolls and trains and toys of all kinds. Jane and Johnny gasped! They walked around the room staring in amazement at all the toys.

"Go on! You can choose whichever toy you want to take back home," he said with a smile.

"Oh, but we can't possibly take anything Sir. We only helped you pick up wood," said Jane stressed.

"Yes, I know, but it's been so long since I've given anything to anyone and since I have a room full of toys and two children who just happened to be passing by that were kind enough to help an old man when they saw he needed it, well, I just had to get you two something, and another thing, you can stop calling me Sir, and start calling me Mr. Muscle," said the old man.

Jane and Johnny looked at each other. "Thank you so much 'Mr. Muscle,' they replied as they smiled with delight.

They looked around the room for the toys that they liked the best. Mr. Muscle smiled as he watched Jane pick up a pretty doll with a bag. His smile grew bigger when he saw Johnny pick up a big aeroplane model. They showed Mr. Muscle what they had picked and they thanked him.

"Mr. Muscle," said Johnny as he carefully put his aeroplane in a bag, "Where did you get all of these toys?" he asked with a frown on his face.

"Well," responded Mr. Muscle, "When you are a toymaker you need to have toys, right?" he said.

Jane and Johnny gasped at the response. "You're a toymaker? It all makes sense now. The wood is used to make toys, why you have so many toys in your house? It is all coming together now!" said Johnny excitedly, then he said with a puzzled look on his face, "Mr. Muscle, if you're a toymaker, aren't you supposed to be selling your toys?" he asked.

Mr. Muscle sighed, "I used to sell my toys once in the village. I was so happy, not because I was earning money, but because I liked to see the happy faces of the children when they got their toys. Sometimes, I would go out and give away my toys for free because I know that there are some who are not so fortunate as the rest and can't afford to buy toys. Everyone loved playing with my toys, but then they started to become more interested in the more modern toys, that they completely forgot about mine. It made me so sad that I moved into the forest," he said sadly.

Jane and Johnny looked at each other and they suddenly had an idea. "Mr. Muscle!" they said excitedly, "We have an idea! Our birthday is nearly coming up and we were planning a big party with balloons and streamers and…. Goodie Bags!" they said.

Mr. Muscle gave a look that showed plain confusion. "Well that's nice but I don't see how…." He suddenly saw what they were trying to say, that if he could make enough toys in time for their birthday, he could give them out as accessories in the goodie bags! If people liked his toys, then he could move back into the village and sell his toys again!

"Oh, I see what you mean. Thank you so much for helping me," he said.

"You're welcome, but we should really be thanking you for these beautiful toys and for helping out with the goodie bags, Mr. Muscle," replied Jane and Johnny.

"My pleasure," said Mr. Muscle happily.

Then they made a few plans for the toys. After a while, when it was time for Jane and Johnny to return to their house, they said their goodbyes to the old man and they left. And when they left, you can be as sure as ever that Mr. Muscle started making toys like he never did before. He made trains, engines, dolls, blocks and much more! He went here and there, painting engines, stitching doll's clothes, perfecting models. He did not stop for a minute and when the day came, everything was ready.

Mr. Muscle was putting the last toy in its box when there came a knock on the door. It was Jane and Johnny!

"Come in," said Mr. Muscle.

Jane and Johnny walked into Mr Muscle's house and weren't they surprised with the sight that awaited them. Toys and toys everywhere! They were all in their boxes, ready to be given out to children coming to the birthday party.

"Mr. Muscle! Thank you so much. They look wonderful!" cried Jane and Johnny admiring the toys.

"Your welcome and Happy Birthday!" replied Mr. Muscle. He took out two gifts; one red, one blue, and gave them to Jane and Johnny.

They smiled with delight "Oh! Mr. Muscle, you really didn't have to, but thank you!" said Jane and Johnny, politely taking the gifts.

They then picked up the toys and put them in some bags that Jane and Johnny had brought with them,"

There were a few other accessories in the bags, they each contained sweets, chocolates, some stickers and a small notepad with pretty designs, but none as nice as Mr. Muscle's toys.

When the party started, you can guess that everyone loved Mr. Muscle's toys. They were all tired with the modern toys so plain and common and yet so expensive. Mr. Muscle was so happy that everyone liked his toys that he moved back into the village and started to sell his toys again.

He was always happy when Jane and Johnny came for vacation and they were his favourite customers. But you can be sure that no one ever picked any other toy over Mr. Muscle's toys again.

POETRY

BY

TIANA

Oh! Ticking Clock

Oh! Ticking clock,

How tired you must be,

Ticking day and night,

On and on for me.

Have a break or go to the zoo,

Maybe we can be late for a day or two.

My door is open,

So, come rest for a while.

But you always seem to have a smile,

Oh! Ticking clock,

How faithful you are,

May I learn from you,

And be a rising star.

THE GREEN BANANA

The green banana I couldn't eat,

I put it in my mouth and it wasn't sweet,

I threw it away for the birds to play.

The banana peel left on the floor,

I slipped and tripped and down I go,

I broke my nose on hitting the door.

So little children please make sure,

don't leave the peel on the floor!

If you care for your nose so dear.

About the Author

Tiana Dora Nongkhlaw

Born on 2nd January 2011 in Shillong, a small city which is the capital of Meghalaya in North East India, Tiana Dora Nongkhlaw has enjoyed books right from a tender age when her mother would read her bedtime stories. Sure enough, when she was able to read, books became her favourite companions. She would often express her dream of living in a house surrounded with books.

In August 2020, Tiana submit her short story "Lost Angel" for a creative writing contest, "Your story Counts," organised by The Hive and Young Author Academy. pWhen the results were announced later that month, Tiana was ecstatic when she heard the news that she was one of the selected winners.

The book "Lost Angel and other stories," was written and completed in November 2020 under the guidance of Annemieke from Young Author Academy.

Besides reading and writing, Tiana enjoys singing and crafts, playing games with her brothers, her cousins and friends. She is currently studying in Class 4 at Loreto Convent Shillong.